W*rd Bird

Story and Pictures by Holcomb Reed

Published by T.T. Potser, Inc.

Moon Man

Anna and Reed

Requests for permission to reproduce any part of this book should be directed to the publisher.
Copies of this book are available in better bookstores or may be ordered from the publisher at

T.T. Potser, Inc.

328 Flatbush Avenue ☀ Suite 167 ☀ Brooklyn, New York 11238
Toll free: (877) 413-2979
Online: www.TTPotser.com
Email: wirdbird@ttpotser.com

Printed on acid free paper in Hong Kong.
Special thanks to Suzy Morris at Creative Printing, USA.

Publisher's Cataloging-in-Publication
(Provided by Quality Books, Inc.)

Reed, Holcomb.
   Wird Bird / story and pictures by Holcomb Reed.
-- 1st ed.
   p. ; cm.
   SUMMARY: A story in verse in which a young parrot hatches and speaks his first word, which is so long and unfamiliar that he must prove its existence in a dictionary.
   LCCN: 99-64438
   ISBN 0-9670198-0-X (library bdg.)
   ISBN 0-9670198-1-8 (hard cover)
   ISBN 0-9670198-2-6 (paperback)

   1. Parrots--Juvenile fiction. 2. Vocabulary-- Juvenile fiction. 3. Birds--Vocalization-- Juvenile fiction. I. Title.

PZ8.3.R2486Wi 1999   [E]
                    QB199-1025

Bayard

Sebastian

Dedicated to

Mark
McGougan

Sharon

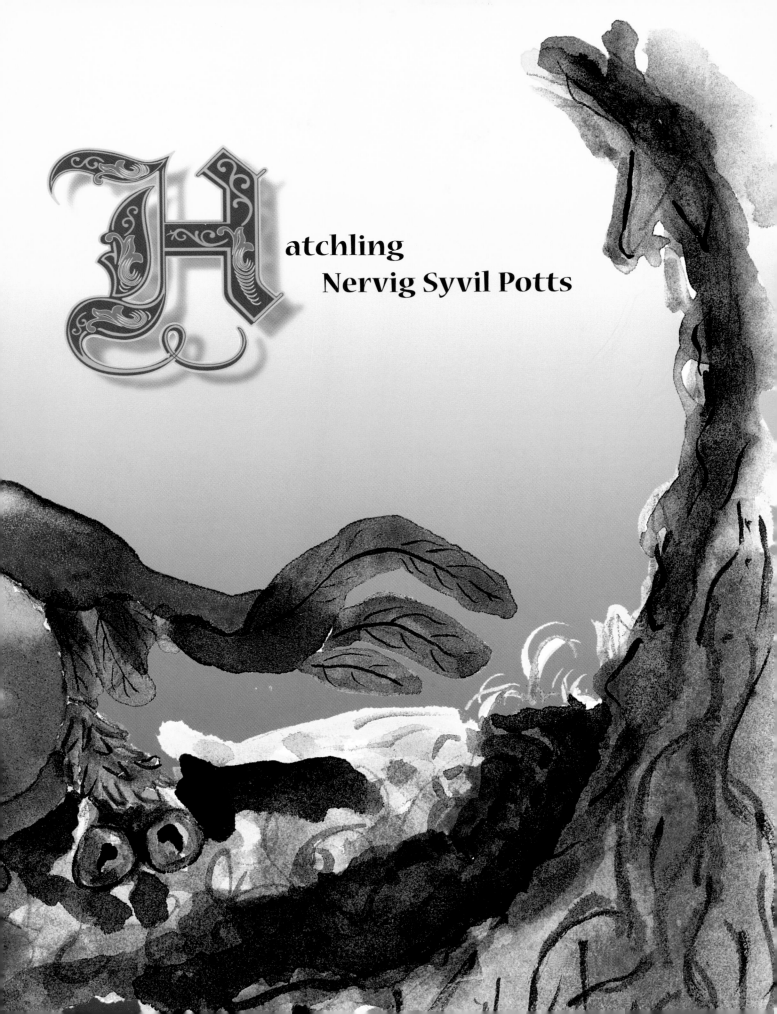

Hatchling
Nervig Syvil Potts

Harrumphed a nest of Polly-Glotts;

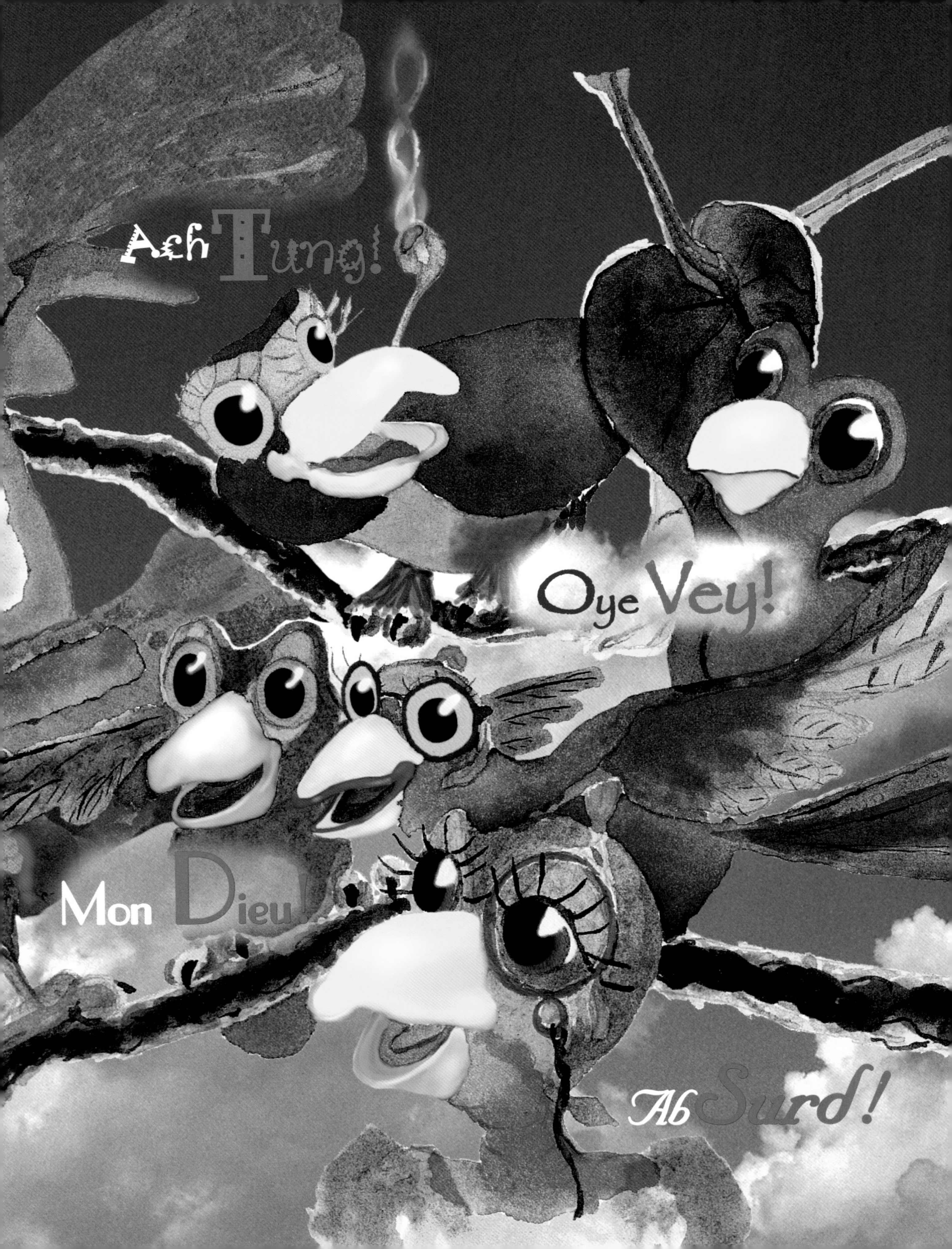
Ach Tung!
Oye Vey!
Mon Dieu!
Ab Surd!

That Nervig used
that what,

that *wird?*

Wird? No, not,
it must be
wrong!

No wird has
ever been so...

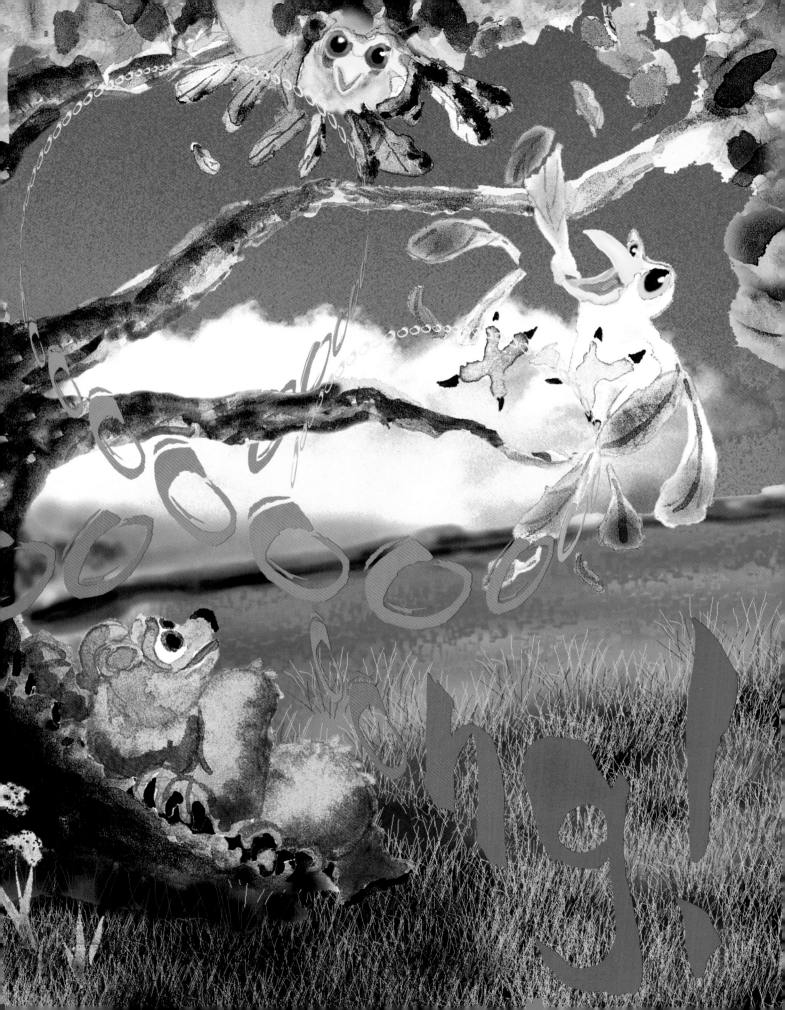

Beak to beak the Glotts conferred,
Not one had ever heard that wird;

They ruffed
through piles
of dictionaries,

Penguins,
Dutch, Gnus,
Canaries...

Polly Anna said, quite shocked,
This wird on earth has ne'er been
SQUAWKED!

Polly Estyr soon concurred,

No warbler's WARBLED near that wird!

No owl had SCREECHED!

No chicken clucked!

No dove had Coooed!

No cowbird moooOed!

No bird Bavarian,

Thai or

Kurd

Had ever *trilled, peeped, chirped* that wird!

It tormented each and every nerd
To hear young Nervig use that wird,
To hear it said with such precision,
A newborn mind in such condition!

And what would Nervig
cheep cheep next?

What kind of bird says

sesquipedalian?

Webster's D
of
Actual English

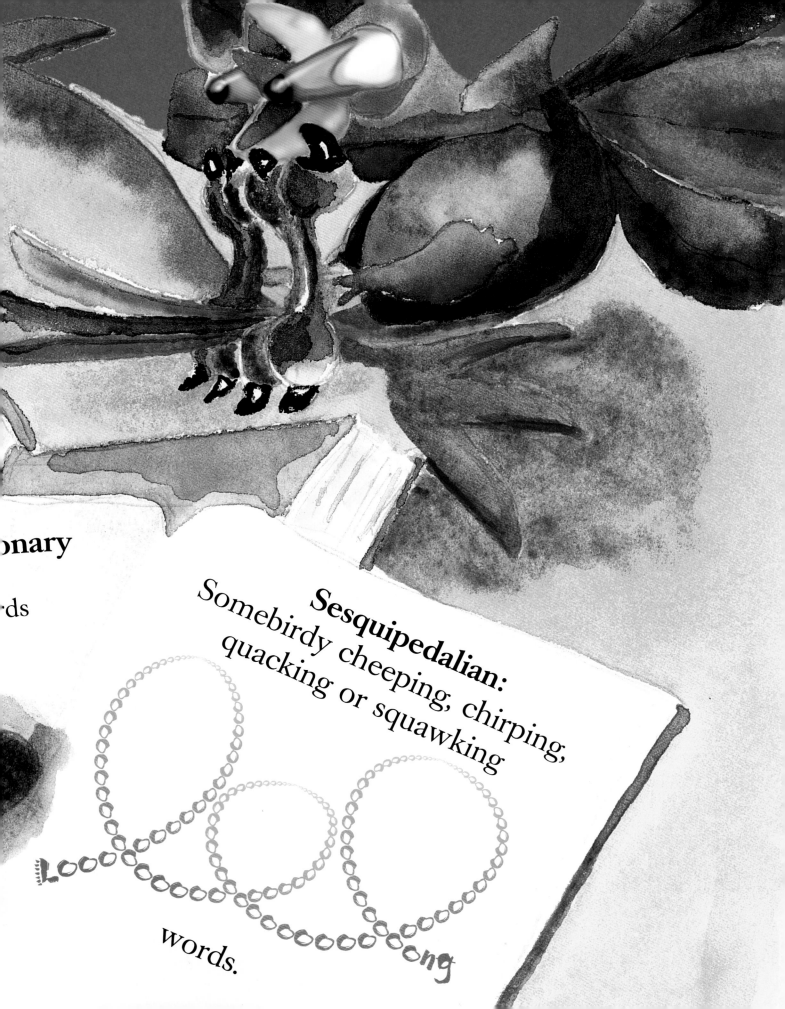

...onary

...rds

Sesquipedalian:
Somebirdy cheeping, chirping,
quacking or squawking

Loooooooooooooooong

words.

Wird Bird, be owl-wise,
Remember the dove;
Polly-Glott? *Loooooong* wirds?
Not!

But,
never short
on love.

Glossary

 Wird Bird - *n.* Anybirdy who says very long wirds. Parrots, myna birds and even ravens have been known to say long wirds. How about you? Are you a wird bird, too?

Hatchling - *n.* A baby that hatches from an egg. Snakes, sea turtles and lizards also hatch from eggs. Can you think of an amphibian that hatches hatchlings? How about an insect? A mammal? An alien?

Polly-Glott - *n.* A parrot (Polly) that speaks every earth language ever spoken. The wird  Polly-Glott is often confused with the English word polyglot (Gk. *Polus,* many + *glòtta,* tongue. Hence, *poluglòttos:* a person who is fluent in many tongues or languages.)

Harrumphed - *v.* Past tense of a wird that was  coined near the end of the last millennium (1949). It indicates distress and disapproval in a pompous sort of way. Harrumphing is done with *know-it-all* throat clearing: *A-he-he-he-HEEEM!*

 **Achtung! Oye Vey! Mon Dieu**! - *interj.* German, Yiddish and French exclamations of distress. English speaking people might cry out, *That's absurd! Gimme a break!* or perhaps, *Fugedaboudit!* How many interjections do you know? How many in a foreign language?

Cowbird - *n.* Some (The Audubon Society) say that the cowbird is a drab, brown bird with a "finch-like bill". Hello?! Anybody home? Forget your *field glasses?* The illustration in the middle has been carefully researched and is udderly accurate.

Bavarian, Thai, Kurd - *n.* People of Europe, Southeast Asia and the Middle East. I could have referred to Canadians or Ukrainians, Easter Islanders, Eskimos or Bedouins, Pennsylvanians or Transylvanians. But the verse only had room for three wirds and Kurd rhymes with wird.

Polly!@#$%^&*!plexed - *adj.* From *Polly,* a name for a parrot and *perplexed* (Lat. per- (intensive) + plectere, to entwine) Intense mental knotting. Bewilderment. The mind entwined is normal among pollyplectuals.

Sesquipedalian - *adj.* From Latin: *sesqui* [*semis,* half + *que,* and.] One and a half. *ped* [*pes,* foot.] Hence, the tendency to use wirds that are a foot and a half *loooooooooooooooooooooooooooooooooooooooooooooooooong.*